The Secret Path of Ned the Ninja

Book Two
Head in the Game

Melissa Mertz
Kea Alwang

The Secret Path of Ned the Ninja: Head in the Game is a work of fiction. Names, characters, places, and incidents are the products of the authors' imaginations or are used fictitiously.

ISBN-13: 978-1500845391
ISBN-10: 1500845396

Library of Congress Control Number: 2014914778

Rounded Star Media, LLC
Paramus, New Jersey
Printed in the United States of America

Contact the authors at:
kea@keaalwang.com
www.nedtheninja.com
www.keaalwang.com

Cover Illustration: C. Spliedt
www.runrabbitproductions.com

Dedicated to:

Those who stand up for others

What the superior man seeks is in himself. What the small man seeks is in others.

- Confucius

Ned's Path so far...

ACKNOWLEDGMENTS

The authors are forever grateful to the following readers of
Ned's first book, *Reluctant Hero* :

Those trusting souls who took a chance on Ned based
on nothing but reviews.

Families at *The Dojo Paramus*

Friends and family who have cheered us on

Elementary school teachers who share Ned
with their students

Uncle Franco
for being our beta reader yet again and
for setting examples of yin yang

CHAPTER ONE

I know. You have questions: Did Ned the Nerd wind up in Witness Protection for standing by as Beck the Bonebreaker kissed the concrete? Did Beck make good on his threat to tackle Ned another day? Did Ned set his coordination-impaired tootsies back on the mats at *Tora Khan Martial Arts*? Did the Tiger King drag our hero out for another night of pushing him beyond his limited limits? Did Ned Herts become the most notable name in superhero comic book history? Did he get the girl?

Before we get ahead of ourselves, let me assure you my limbs, neck, and spine are still in one awkward piece. That said, Jared Beck greets me with the snarling glares of a rabid mountain lion several times a day, every day. Don't get me wrong: I *am* grateful Beck hasn't come within six feet of me. It's just tough going about my day waiting for that mountain lion to pounce. (Just between us, I carry extra underwear in my backpack in case ... well, you know.)

And karate? I did return for a second class. But this time, instead of fighting my parents on the way in, I bolted through the front door of *Tora Khan Martial Arts*.

Sensei Melissa noticed and exclaimed, "Ned! I'm so glad you're excited to return for another lesson!"

Excited? Try desperate to escape my mother's attempt at a good luck, smoochie-woochie smother fest just as students Greg Spencer, Julian Cobb, and Adrianna Ronan crossed the parking lot behind us. Worried Mom would try again inside the lobby, I raced by Sensei as quickly as possible, leaving her to intercept the helicopter that is my mother. Poor Sensei Melissa: I bet she can sense attacks coming from any direction. Still, when Mom lured her in with a simple question about tuition, my teacher probably didn't suspect what was to follow. Mom suddenly pulled out the school handbook to make sure she understood everything in it. The situation had me giggling silently as I pushed my shoes into a cubbie. But then I heard Sensei explain that her art has *eleven* kicks to master. I gulped. Yes, I had come back for a second class voluntarily, but did I really want eleven new ways to fall on my butt? Eleven new ways to have that butt kicked? Not so much.

But before I start whining, let's begin our story at my most recent class, two weeks after my first....

During warm-up, my Jumping Jills finally became Jumping Jacks. Bravo, Ned? Maybe—but let's not forget that Jack, the dude that fell and broke his crown on some hill right in front of a girl, wasn't known for his coordination skills, either.

When Sensei counted out push-ups in Japanese, I tried to focus on the strange words instead of pain shooting through the overcooked spaghetti most people call arms. Mind over matter, right? *Ichi! Ni! San,* came the count. Sensei loves a good push-up, so I tried my best to control the bend in my elbows to avoid a face-plant. For every push-up I did, the rest of the class did three. Still, that's better than the last class when everyone did five for each of mine.

My splits went no lower today, but at least they didn't hurt anybody. Adrianna, the orange belt with the orange hair, kept looking at me from over her shoulder while she sat in a perfect split. Noticing this caused throwing stars to fly around in my stomach, but I had to face reality: Even though she smiled at me, Adrianna's glances were all about self-preservation. Get kicked once in the head by a dork, you need to keep an eye on the dork. I couldn't blame her.

"Fighting stance!" Sensei called. I stumbled to my feet and into a fighting stance: one foot forward, bent at the knee, back leg straight. I raised both fists to protect my face.

"Herts!" Sensei called.

"Yes, Sensei?"

"Are you trying to break your thumbs?"

What kind of question was that? Why not ask me if I'd like to rip off my ears or run my pancreas through a fax machine?

"No, Sensei?"

Adrianna forced open each of my hands and pulled out the thumbs, which I had tucked inside.

"Thank you, Adrianna," said Sensei. "Now please explain what Ned did wrong. How would you teach him to make a proper fist?"

Adrianna held her palms open toward me, so I copied her. "Curl in your fingers," she said in a voice that could make angels jealous. Then she curved her fingers into her palms until I couldn't see her fingernails. "Now place your thumbs on the *outside* of your fist. Many arts hook the thumbs around the fist at the side, but our art places them on top ... like this. See how the thumb knuckle sticks up? Never, never tuck the thumbs inside your fist; you could break them if you punch hard enough."

I bent my thumbs at the knuckles and rested the tips on top of my fists.

"Push down with your thumbs, Ned," Sensei added.

"Because you'll have stronger punches!" Greg Spencer called out.

"Correct, Mr. Spencer, but you're calling out," Sensei said.

"Grrr ... hurummmpff ... oo," Julian muttered beside me. Translation: *Like that's a surprise?* Then he glanced at my thumbs and nodded his approval, adding, "Grr ... murrph ... wrrrump!"

"Really?" I wondered out loud.

"What's so jaw dropping, Herts?" Sensei asked.

"Julian just told me the thumb knuckle on top also acts as a weapon?"

"It can," Sensei said with a firm nod. "But you'll be a much higher rank before we explore that."

I tried to wipe a sudden grin from my face—not because I liked the idea of beating up someone using only my thumb knuckles, but because I felt like one of those superhero mutants whose weapons suddenly grew out of their bodies. Immediately, my mind went to work outfitting one of my custom comic book characters with crazy tools that erupt from his thumbs at a moment's notice: mini torpedoes, magnifying glass, compass, screwdriver, camera ... toothpick?

A foot whipped out beside me. Back to reality: One glance

at the mirrors told me the entire class was drilling front snap kicks while I stood there with a dreamy, ridiculous look on my face.

"Herts! Wake up. I want to see front snap kicks that actually snap!" Sensei instructed. "The knee should lift first, the ball of the foot must come straight at me, toes pulled back."

I knew all that from my last class: The ball of the foot sits right under the big toe and should make contact with a target. A kick goes as high as your knee lifts. Unfortunately, understanding the technique doesn't mean I have the coordination to pull it off.

"Ichi!" Sensei counted in Japanese.

I kicked, pulling my toes back.

"Ni!"

I focused on lifting my knee higher this time ... and pitched sideways into Adrianna who grabbed my elbow to steady me. Back in my fighting stance, I shut my eyes so I wouldn't have to watch the flailing jellyfish in the mirror.

"San!"

I kicked high and didn't fall. Tora Khan was right; sight *is* my weakest sense. Apparently, I'm better off when I can't see what I'm doing. Note to self: Quirk #382 ... better off blind.

"Herts! Keep your fists up in front of you to protect your face. Don't flail them around as if they're chicken wings."

Lady, this chicken is mighty proud of his wings.

"Shi!"

That would be number four. How many kicks were we doing? Eyes still closed, I focused on keeping my fists in front of me.

"Nice, Herts! Excellent job using the ball of the foot. Beautiful technique."

I nodded at the compliment, too shocked to speak. Finally ... a physical activity where I can make someone else afraid of the ball.

"Horse stance!" Sensei called.

I jumped into a horse stance: feet apart, knees bent, fists placed upside down on my waist.

Sensei Melissa took a deep breath. "I want to review an important martial arts concept today. We have younger ranks in this class," she nodded toward Adrianna and me, "and I want to make sure each one of you understands how ranking works—and how it does not work."

"Rank follows the man!" James Dorchester blurted. "That's what you always say."

"Which means what?" Sensei asked.

Dorchester shrugged, then giggled. "I don't know. I just always thought it sounded cool."

Peter Austin raised his hand like a proper purple belt. "It means if you're a black belt, it's more important you act like a black belt than the fact that you are one?"

"Exactly," Sensei smiled. "But I overheard something sad the other day while walking by students from another martial arts school. I want to make sure my students know better."

"Aww ..." said Dorchester, his face long and sympathetic. "What happened, Sensei?"

"I saw four Junior Black Belts in a shouting match over who was the best among them versus who did not deserve their rank."

The class stood silently.

"Julian Cobb, James Dorchester, and Maya Kimura, step forward, please."

The three blue belts took their horse stances front and center.

Sensei took a deep breath. "What is Mr. Cobb's greatest martial arts quality?"

Clara Wheaton raised her hand. "His stances. They are always low and balanced. You never have to remind him to bend his knees."

Sensei nodded. "Agreed. And Mr. Dorchester's?"

"His energy," Adrianna answered. "He's super fast and never seems to get tired."

"And Ms. Kimura?"

"Her punches," said Greg. "I hate holding shields for her. My arms hurt the next day."

"All blue belts. Each has at least one strength. And if you asked about weaknesses, they would have them, too. Each of these students deserves the belt they wear, no matter how they perform any particular skill compared to the students next to them. Each student walks his own path in this school and throughout life. My job is to decide whether a student's physical and mental skills grew stronger since the last time he tested for a new rank."

Dorchester, beaming, said, "That's why I love karate. I don't have to be a mega athlete or look like The Incredible Hulk, because..." he held up a very skinny arm to show his muscles, "I'm not!"

The class laughed, but not nastily.

"And I might not be a genius," Dorchester raised a finger in the air. "But Adrianna's right: I *am* fast."

"Lightning fast," said Lucas Clemens.

Clara raised her hand. "I'm fast too, but not for long, because then I'll need my inhaler. But I can jump high."

"High? You're like a rocket!" Adrianna laughed.

I leaned toward Adrianna to whisper, "Why does she need an inhaler?"

"Asthma," she replied.

I nearly choked. "Her?" I asked in awe.

Adrianna just nodded.

"What about Ned?" Sensei suddenly asked. "Can we find a strength in Ned yet?"

Tell me she didn't ask that.

"Nah," said Greg. "He's just a white belt."

My face turned a strange red in the mirrored wall before us. The shade deserved a spot in crayon boxes as 'Embarrassed Lobster Red.'

Adrianna's cute little face scrunched fiercely as she turned in Greg's direction, but Julian spoke first. And what he said was only slightly less amazing than how he said it—loud and almost clear: "I have never seen a new student try as hard as Ned does. He has something called...."

"Heart!" Clara finished for him. "Ned has heart."

"I agree," Sensei said with a huge smile. "When he falls, he gets up and moves forward. We all have unique challenges. Ned meets his head-on ... sometimes literally ... but he doesn't give up, however fast or slow he moves along his path. And that sort of determination reflects the heart and soul of a true martial artist."

My cheeks went from Embarrassed Lobster Red to a new

color: Bashful Crimson Pride. Certainly, I had the muscle tone of a sock, the flexibility of a brick, the balance of a lollipop, and sometimes a nasty case of eczema, but I had heart, too. I, Ned Herts, had heart.

CHAPTER TWO

After four rounds of punching drills (thumbs in their rightful place), Sensei jogged backward to the lower-rank end of the room until she stood in front of me. "Can anyone explain 'kata' to Ned?" she asked.

"Form exercise," Greg blurted, clearly in a hurry to answer before anyone else.

"Yes," said Sensei Melissa, "but how do we explain that to a white belt?"

Lucas pulled both ends of his belt to tighten the knot and

answered, "Kata is a series of upper- and lower-body moves done in sequences that we memorize. These sequences are used to train the body to react quickly and to drill proper technique. We have eight hand katas in our art, Sensei."

"Beautiful, Mr. Clemens. And what is Kata number one called?"

"Seisan, Sensei!" Greg shouted confidently. Then he leaned forward to stare down the line at me and said, "That's saaay saaahhhhhn, White Belt!"

Say what?

"And its other name?" Sensei asked.

Clara's hand shot up, but Greg's mouth was faster. "It's the Half Moon Kata, Sensei!"

Dorchester raised his hand, swaying side to side.

"Yes, Mr. Dorchester?"

"Can you imagine what a Full Moon Kata looks like?"

Sensei opened her mouth, then closed it. Finally, she said, "I don't even know how to answer that, Dorchester. But tell me, how many parts are there to Seisan Kata?"

"Four," Dorchester held up four fingers.

"And how many moves in the entire kata?"

"One hundred and thirty."

"And how long should it take to run through the kata?"

"One minute, Sensei."

"Thank you, Mr. Dorchester, for discussing *important* information with us."

Dorchester flashed his lopsided grin. "You're always welcome, Sensei. But I still wonder—"

"And who," Sensei moved on before Dorchester could ramble, "can tell me how many people Seisan teaches us to fight?"

Peter raised his hand. "Thirteen, Sensei."

I let out a lung-emptying gasp. In fact, it took a nudge from Adrianna to get me breathing again. Thirteen attackers? All at once? Unlucky number. Unlucky martial artist.

Sensei looked amused. "Okay there, Ned?"

"Um ... yes, Sensei?" lied this boy who could be pinned against a wall by thirteen dirty *looks*. And right there, I began to imagine Jared Beck and twelve clones fitted with hi-tech armor, their punches reinforced by thrusters at the elbows,

16

headgear and forearm shields covered in metal spikes. Suddenly, all at once, they rush me to—

"Are you with me, Ned? We start Seisan with our heels together and our toes apart, feet in the letter 'V'. Just follow along as best you can. You'll learn how to 'speak' the movements as I speak them, do them as I do them. In this way, our art passes from teacher to student, from generation to generation."

So I attempted to make my feet and arms follow a bunch of weird moves on command while my lips silently repeated the words with the class:

Bow, hammer, shield, two hammers—

Was I learning karate in a dojo or a tool shed?

Step, block, punch, block, step, punch, block....

The moves were like a dance, and I wondered how this kata thing would defend me against Beck. I mean why not do the *Macarena* or the *Hokey Pokey* the next time he corners me in the schoolyard? I'd probably get the same results.

Shutos down, put 'em on your obi....

"Herts! Your obi is your belt, remember? Not your rib

MERTZ / ALWANG

cage. You look like a frightened chicken."

Again with the chicken insults? What did this lady have against my fine feathered friends? I moved my spear hands down to my belt. "But Sensei," I said out loud, forgetting myself, "If I'm fighting thirteen people, I *am* scared and you can bet I'm a chicken."

Even though she ignored my comment, I could swear Sensei fought a smile. Julian snorfled as my face pinked in the mirror once more. "Good one," he mumbled.

Step, shutos high and low, strike 'em, grab 'em ... throw 'em to the ground!

My chin hit the mats. The class halted, and Sensei appeared at my side instantly.

"Ned! Are you okay?" She helped me sit up.

I pushed my jaw side to side, up and down. "I think so."

"What happened?"

"You said, throw him to the ground."

Clearly flustered, as any intelligent person would be, Sensei said, "You throw *your opponent* to the ground."

"I see that now. But landing on the ground is usually *my*

role in a fight. Guess I went on autopilot."

Palm to forehead, Sensei motioned for me to stand. "Class, let's take it from the beginning of part two."

Julian leaned behind Adrianna to tell me, "Gguuddd, grre hruso bup."

What Julian said, "Dude, that was messed up," really sucker punched me. He didn't say it in a mean way, either. More like a 'you poor, pathetic, lutz' sort of way. The comment made me set my jaw in fierce determination, because you know what? If thirteen guys ever do come at me, the last thing they'll throw at me is pity. So I dusted myself off and lived through part two, then three, then four of Seisan. After several run-throughs, Sensei had us sit, hands on knees, around her.

"Remember," she said, "whenever it becomes necessary to defend yourself, you'll have a harder time if your opponent takes you by surprise. In other words, always be aware of your surroundings. A good martial artist can sense a threat close by. He or she projects what we might think of as a force field of energy created by confident body language, awareness, and intuition.

"Does everyone understand what I mean by intuition? Intuition is knowledge that comes to you without evidence ... without knowing something for sure. Our five senses—seeing, hearing, smelling, feeling, tasting—kick into gear over things we know exist. We can see a strawberry, smell it, touch it, taste it—it is there. Our skin reacts to the wind, to a change in temperature. But intuition is a sixth sense, something we know in our gut, even if we don't know *how* we know it. The trick is to learn to pay attention to our intuition and eventually trust it.

"More importantly, martial artists do their best not to fall into risky situations before they even need their intuition. For example, at your age, should you walk home alone, at night, through a lonely part of town?"

"No, Sensei!" Greg Spencer replied like a soldier.

"Sensei," Peter raised his hand, "that's just asking for trouble."

"Exactly." Sensei raised a finger. "But let's say you didn't use your common sense and walked home alone, anyway. If you were in touch with your intuition, you would sense trouble as it approached."

Sensei was telling *me* about sensing trouble? Ha! I can sense Beck the Bonebreaker within twenty-five feet of me. It *is* almost like a force field. Not the type that keeps things from touching me, unfortunately, but one could call it 'Bonebreaker radar.' I'm ready the moment that guy steps into my 'force field.' Ready to run, hide, maybe walk closer to a teacher or lunch aide. Go ahead and laugh, but those tactics have kept me alive. Not sure what would happen if I started kata-ing all over Beck.

I watched Sensei carefully as she went on about unavoidable versus avoidable bad situations, and I wondered: What was her force field like? Would weapons bounce off it?

"Books! Bags! Bos!" Sensei suddenly boomed, commanding us to prepare for the end of class.

Everyone scrambled to pull fat equipment bags from the side of the room. They yanked wooden sticks called bos from a rack on the wall. After returning to a floor dot, each student pulled a small notepad from his bag. Sounds simple, right?

Not so much. All the bags looked the same, so I had trouble finding mine. Since I hadn't bought protective fighting gear yet, my bag should have been skinnier and easier to spot. But because my mom is ... well, my mom, my bag was just as fat with a first-aid kit, a change of underclothes (so I didn't have to go home sweaty), and four bottles of water I never use because we aren't allowed to drink or eat around the mats. Yes, I do have a unique key chain I could hook onto the bag's handle. No, I won't use it; the only one my mother had was a tiny stuffed blue bear. I told her forget it. She pointed out blue is for boys. I said, "Yeah. Blue for boys, mom. They make blue dresses, too. Should I wear one of those?"

Once I found the bag, I dragged it back to my dot. (Anyone need enough gauze and bandages to treat a sixteen-car pile up?) I dug through everything, searching for my notepad, called a time book—the most important piece of karate gear I own. After each class, Sensei uses it to track time toward our next rank.

"Sensei!" yelled Dorchester, "What section in our books?"

"Self-defense," said Sensei Melissa from the high-rank end

of the line. As she wrote time into Peter's book, she added, "And if you helped me with the younger class earlier, be sure to ask for your Assistant Teaching time."

I'd bet real money that Japan would have to float across the Pacific Ocean to hang out with California before Sensei would ask me to teach anyone anything. That time must be important, though: I noticed Greg asked Sensei for his Assistant Teaching time as if he were getting candy.

When I finally yanked my book free of the bag, the hachikama Tora Khan gave me fell out with it. I kept meaning to wear it in class, but nobody else wears one, so I'm too shy to use it.

"Herts!" Sensei's voice came from right behind me. Wasn't she just at the opposite end of the room? "What do you have there?"

I gulped. Would she make me wear it now that she has seen it? "It's my hachikama," I said, trying to sound like the strip of material was no big deal.

Silence. Sensei stared down at me, a cautious expression crossing her face.

"Sensei?"

"Herts, that strip of cloth is called a *hachimaki* ... not a hachikama." Her voice was low, puzzled.

But Tora Khan had called it a hachikama. What was that about? Unfortunately, I couldn't ask Sensei straight out. I mean, it's just weird to ask your teacher if her father shows up in the middle of the night to tutor klutzy nerds in martial arts. Actually, at my last class, I tried to get more information about the man by way of questions that sounded innocent enough. It was no use, though; none of Sensei's answers revealed a thing about Tora Khan.

I had asked, "So does your father like your dojo?"

She said, "I hope so."

Another time, when I asked if Tora Khan outranked her, she just said, "Always."

And when I asked if he still teaches her, she said, "A martial artist never stops learning."

"Well," I dared, "Does he ever show up here?"

"All the time," was her answer.

Sensei gently took the hachimaki from me and ran a

thumb over the emblem. "That's the Siberian Tiger on it, huh? My father's teacher, known as the Siberian Tiger, would have liked it."

I bit my tongue before I could say, "Yeah, I know."

"You should wear it in class some time."

"Yes, Sensei."

CHAPTER THREE

"So ... uh, Ned Herts to Tora Khan! Come in, Tora Khan!" I called out while alone in my bedroom. "Yo! Tora Khan!"

Nothing. I picked up a pencil and began doodling in my sketch book. I used to draw plenty of trademarked superheroes. These days, I've doubled my efforts creating my own guys. After all, I'm me, so I have my own ideas, right? For example, the lead guy in my superhero universe, Magnovitacious the Monumental, has a wimpy body, battles breathing problems, and suffers from a terrible dairy allergy. But get him angry?

26

Mess with his friends? You're going *down*, buddy! Yeah, the name, Magnovitacious is a mouthful. But that won't matter because, before long, it will be on every self-respecting comic geek's lips.

Abruptly, I dropped my pencil.

"Seriously?" I whisper-hissed at the ceiling, "You show up *once*, just long enough to make me think I'm suffering from the crazies. Sure, I have the black gi you gave me. And I have this blindfold thingie..." I stuck a finger beneath the hachi-whatever-it's-called to scratch my forehead, "but other than that? Just a whole bunch of questions. Are you ever going to show up again?"

Nothing.

I jumped from my desk, pushed my glasses further up my nose, and stood in the middle of my room. "Hey, guy ... look!" I placed my feet in the letter 'V' and began my Seisan kata. "Bow, hammer, wrench, shield, two hammers, throw my arms on up ... break it on down. Catch fists together. Huh ... I forget what I'm supposed to do with my hands there. Well, anyway," I cleared my throat, "Shutos down, obi, step, hi and hello, strike 'em, grab 'em, throw 'em to the ground ... by the way, I should stay on my feet at that point ... put my hands back on my obi—as if they'll do me any good there."

I stomped my feet back together, side by side, and glared at the ceiling. "Hey!" I shouted. "Let's face facts: My kata stinks! Shouldn't you swing by and fix it? I move around like a cartoon character who just got slammed on the head with a golf club."

My door flew open. "Ned?" Mom stepped into my room cautiously, followed by Cracker Jack. "Who are you talking to?"

"Nobody. Just practicing my karate kata."

Mom placed her hands on her hips, shook her head with a smile. "Your father and I are so proud of how well you're doing. And you didn't want to try karate!"

As if I had a choice. Either I learned to defend myself or Beck would eventually use me as a portable punching bag on legs. Besides, who wanted to sit through more of Dad's lectures?

"Oh Ned, don't look so sour. I know, nobody wants to hear, 'I told you so.' I'm sorry."

"It's okay," I yawned, then snapped my sketch book shut.

Mom pursed her lips. "I hate to ask, but shouldn't you give that bandana to me to wash? You're always wearing it around the house. You're not sleeping in it are you?"

"No." Yes, I was—every night. My fingers moved to the cloth around my head. "It's fine. I like wearing it. I'll let you know when it smells."

Mom shrugged. "Not if I let you know first. I hope karate isn't going to turn you into one of those stinky boys who never shower."

"You mean instead of smelling like that lavender soap and strawberry-scented shampoo you buy? I hope so."

Mom grinned, clearly thinking I made a funny. "My silly boy. You know the products we buy are one-hundred-percent all natural and organic. How can you go wrong? No toxic ingredients for my family!"

"'Course not, Mom," I sighed. One day I'll have a job and buy my own bath products, so I smell like a man. For now, it's a miracle nobody calls me Ned the Nostril Nuisance.

Mom asked, "Can you take Cracker Jack for a walk before you settle in for the night? He's not having the best day, and he seems to perk up when you walk him."

I looked down at my hound. Poor Cracker Jack, forever cursed with droopy eyes that made it seem as if he wished someone would give him a break all day, every day. How could anyone tell his good days from the bad? "Come on, boy!" I said, scooping him into my arms. "Let's take that walk. I'll bring you to the corner mailbox and back."

For most Kolleti Street residents, a trip to the mailbox takes between thirty seconds and four minutes, depending on how far you live up the street. Because I took my usual path all the way around the block to avoid passing Jared Beck's house, it would take Cracker Jack and me nearly thirty minutes, there and back. Even if I didn't worry about what Beck would do to me, his dog —Bob, a bulldog with an attitude problem—makes my dog piddle in fear. Sometimes I think Cracker Jack and I were separated at birth.

As we made our way around the corner at the top of the street, then began to pass the edge of the small forest that runs between my street and the next, Cracker Jack seemed to perk up. He even pulled at his leash a few times, and I—in no rush— let him sniff around at whatever he liked. Then it hit me: I have a hound! What do hounds do? They pick up scents.

I pulled the hachi-kama-maki from my head, thinking it might still have Tora Khan's scent on it. Would Cracker Jack know what to do with it?

The hound gave me a put-upon stare, then hesitantly moved his nose closer to the cloth. One sniff and he backed away five paces faster than I'd seen him move in a long time.

"Come on, boy." I pushed the cloth back at him.

Cracker Jack whined, then threw back his head and howled. Apparently, Mom was right: I had become a gross sort of boy. Maybe I should start wearing deodorant—on my forehead.

"Let's go, Jackie Man. How about we jog the rest of the way? Come on, boy!"

I should have known better. The instant I tried to run, Cracker Jack pulled against his leash, the fur on his neck stood straight, and his paws shuffled to grip the sidewalk. As I encouraged him the way Mom does, with baby talk, the fur on *my* neck prickled unexpectedly. Slowly, I turned to face a car trailing alongside us.

The driver, a woman with curly blonde hair, craned her neck out the window to stare at me. "Hey, Jared. Is that the Herts boy?" She sounded angry.

Jared Beck, sitting in the backseat, sneered out his window at me, his face a super storm of anger. "Yeah, that's him. So what?"

"Cute dog you have there!" Beck's mom called, her voice suddenly sugar. "You're the smart kid in Jared's grade, right?"

"I guess," I choked, knees knocking. Did she think that was a good or bad thing?

"Well, my kid? He's not so bright. Short on the academics, know what I mean? Jared just got another twenty-five on a math test, so I've been thinking I should get him a tutor. But he's going to need lots of help. Think you're up for the job?"

Surprised my eyeballs had not popped from their sockets and rolled under Mrs. Beck's car, I glanced at The Bonebreaker. Without one word, his expression demanded that I say, 'no way, no how.'" My thoughts exactly.

"Speak up, kid," Mrs. Beck sighed. "Do you want the job or not? I have to get genius here to a dental appointment before that brownish tooth causes an infection."

I shrugged, simply because I could not speak. I laughed a nervous laugh that quickly became hiccups. Then I nearly threw up when Jared shook his fist at me.

"You sure that's the smart one?" Jared's mom tossed back at him. To me, she said, "I'll just talk to the school." As the car pulled away, she added, "Enjoy your evening!" Yeah, because that would happen now.

I gave in to jelly legs and sat on the sidewalk wondering what was worse: tutoring Beck, imagining what Beck would do to me if I did, or having a Mom who puts her kid down in front of another kid. Maybe living with a mother who shines a flashlight in your mouth once week to check for suspect cavities is better than one who doesn't care about your teeth until they turn brown.

Suddenly, it seemed a little easier to have a mom who is part mother and part 'smother' than to live with a hands-off parent like Jared's. Some people say bullies bully because they are missing something in their lives. Maybe Beck needed a nicer mom....

CHAPTER FOUR

6 6 Whatever you do," warned Tommy Douglas, "don't tell your mom that Mrs. Beck wants you to tutor the Bonebreaker. Maybe she'll forget. Maybe the guidance counselor will suggest someone else. If you bring it up to your Mom, she'll think it's a great opportunity and make you do it."

"Good point," I said as we walked into the gym. Tom was the only friend I could rely on at Pascack Brook Elementary. For one thing, he knew the importance of flying below Beck's radar. "Man, I can't wait until the day we start our mega-entertainment company," I gushed. "*We* will call all the shots."

"I don't know," Tom wiggled his allergy-prone nose. "If I do go into the gaming and comic book business with you, what will my position be?"

I rolled my eyes. "Vice President, obviously!"

"But of what?" Tom poked my shoulder with one finger. "Vice President of Video-Game Creation?"

"Sure," I told him. I mean like he's going to remember me promising him that fifteen years from now? I didn't have the heart to tell him that Huck Fortunado—the primo video-game designer in the industry—would get that job once Tom and I made enough moolah to float Huck's crazy salary. Honestly? I wanted Tom to run Marketing. He's an idea man.

"Yikes," said Tom, stopping short. "Looks like Mr. Hicks is picking captains for teams. Whatever you do, don't call attention to yourself."

My heart and stomach raced each other to my feet. "Funny. I didn't see 'Nerd Torture Day' on the calendar," I whispered.

"Every day is Nerd Torture Day around here," Tom pouted. "Okay, Ned. You know what to do. I'll take the wall. You take the bleachers today. Whatever you do, give it your best Oscar-winning performance."

"Right." I ran to the opposite side of the gym before Mr. Hicks could call the class to attention. Unfortunately, I didn't notice the 'Wet Paint–Do Not Climb' sign hung across the bleachers until I got there. I turned around just in time to watch Tom attempt to dribble a basketball. He looked down until ... *smack!* His head appeared to slam into the wall. He fell backward with a moan that echoed through the gym. Don't worry though; the smack came from a discreet stomp of his foot. Tom was fine (he takes stage combat classes), his performance better than the one I pulled off with that same routine last month.

"Ohhhh, my head!" Tom moaned as Mr. Hicks ran over. "Is it cracked like a hard-boiled egg? Will I die? Whatever you do, tell my parents I love them!"

Tom, man: Don't overdo it.

For his stellar performance, Tom won a pass to the nurse where he would receive an icepack and a pep talk before returning to *watch* gym class. On his way out of the gym, he swayed left and right as if disoriented and threw me a thumbs-up when nobody was looking.

Yeah. Thumbs-up for *him.* My dramatic performance of tripping down the bleachers had been canceled. I was stuck, doomed ... destined for last pick on a team once again.

Mr. Hicks blew his whistle and gathered us around the team captains, Carolina Sapienza and Jared Beck. "The name of the game is *Capture the Flag*! Listen for your name, then head over to your team."

The choosing process was no surprise. Mr. Hicks believed in 'ladies first,' so Carolina had first pick. With twenty-four students in the class, minus Tommy, Carolina would get the final pick. Since I'm always everyone's last pick, I would wind up on Carolina's team. Whew! At least Beck wouldn't own me today.

Still, the Bonebreaker would make tagging me his first move of the game. He always did, with a strategy that involved getting one of his friends on my team to 'accidentally' trip me. Once that happens, Beck runs from behind to pounce as I go down— appearing to innocently trip over me. And without fail, one of his elbows digs into my ribs when he lands. Recently, I learned to avoid his strategy with one of my own: I make it easy for someone else to tag me first, seconds into the game, then spend the rest of gym class safely in the other team's jail. I wind up last guy onto a team, first guy off. It works for me.

Just as the captains were almost finished choosing, Tommy returned. As he headed for Mr. Hicks, I noticed something frightening: He was not holding an excuse pass. After a word with Mr. Hicks, he came to stand beside me.

"What happened?" I asked.

"Substitute nurse," huffed Tom as he twitched at the neck. "She told me I'd be fine."

"That's malpractice!" I said, quickly running the team odds through my head again.

"She said she is more 'tough love' than Mrs. Sedhu and that today's boys need to toughen up."

"Or maybe today's nurse just needs a soul," I muttered.

So the captains' last two picks came down to me and Tom. Carolina would choose one of us, Jared would get the leftovers. Would my chances of winding up on Carolina's team fall to a simple fifty/fifty shot? Hardly. No, there was one more factor to consider, and it had nothing to do with numbers logic: Tom lent Carolina his science textbook last week when she forgot hers at home. That had to count for something.

Carolina's big brown eyes weighed the decision over me and Tom as if she had to choose between a spoon and a salt shaker for fixing a leaky faucet. Finally, her finger pointed at Tom, as I suspected it would, placing me on Jared's team.

Carolina's team nodded its approval. Believe it or not, the outcome of weighing the lesser of two nerds used to favor me. Apparently, I lost my edge when Tommy stopped digging at his nose during games.

"Circle up!" Jared shouted to his team.

So we circled up, and Jared ordered each kid to play either offense or defense—each kid, but me. And I certainly wasn't going to ask about my role.

I glanced at the kids on the other team. All smiles and laughter, they interacted with Carolina as if she were one of them—not a 'win at all costs' dictator. Even Tom had lost his neck twitch. By comparison, my team looked edgy, uptight. They knew the score: Mess up on Jared's team and the Bonebreaker got mean.

"The game will go down like this," Beck began. "Ned the Nerd here will be tagged out in seconds, as usual. Nobody rescue him from the other team's jail. We have a better chance of winning without him. Once he's out of the way...."

I wanted to cry, so I stared at the gym floor. Beck spoke about me as if I were one big invisible nothing. Of course, if I really was invisible, I'd be worth something to my team. I could sneak into the other team's territory to steal their flag, and they would never see me coming—

A super-loud gasp popped out of my mouth as a strategy for winning the game popped into my head. When I looked up from the floor, I realized I wasn't invisible after all, because my team suddenly took notice of me. Would anyone listen to my idea? I knew Beck wouldn't.

"You got something to say, Nerd?" Beck asked, hands on hips, sneer on lips.

Without a hachimaki to shield me from Beck's nasty glare, I didn't stand a chance of getting words out of my mouth. So I turned slightly left to face Bobby Trayman—a less threatening sort of guy. Bobby looked doubtful, but at least he didn't seem ready to pummel me.

I cleared my throat. "Since I wind up tagged and in jail within the first five minutes of the game every time, maybe ... maybe I should put myself there."

Beck cackled. "Whatever Nerd. Get tagged or put yourself there. Who cares as long as you're out of the way."

"But ... if I'm in there without really getting tagged ... then I'm not really in jail. But everyone will think I'm there because someone tagged me. They'll think that because that's what always happens to me. But I could *leave* jail because I *wasn't* really tagged. So...."

"So ..." Bobby got excited, "Ned could easily grab the flag, which will be somewhere near the jail! He'll be a spy behind enemy lines. Ned, that just might work."

Jared's face clouded. "No, it won't. It's a stupid plan."

"It's worth a try," said Bobby, and three more players nodded.

Mary Gibbons said, "A bunch of us could cause chaos as he moves into position."

"He'll blow it!" Jared hissed.

Bobby got in Jared's face. "You're going to blow it if you keep getting loud. The other team will hear you."

It wasn't long before our team had pressured Jared into trying my idea. Mary rolled her eyes at him impatiently. Bobby kept lashing out with, "Come on, Man!" Zack, the shortest kid in the fifth grade whispered, "Bobby's right." Naomi, hands on hips, said, "Everyone deserves a chance to prove themselves."

41

(Always liked Naomi.) And even Christoper, one of Beck's sidekicks said, "Jared, it's a different sort of idea. If it doesn't work, we can always hang him by his underwear from the schoolyard fence." Did this many people really have my back? Way to go, Herts! Still, Christopher made a good point: If the plan nose-dived, Beck would target me worse than before. I felt a wedgie coming on.

As Zack built our team's 'jail' with huge puzzle mats, and Mary planted our 'flag' (an orange cone) near the rock wall on our half of the gym, Jared Beck focused on his career as Chief Bully by mushing one finger into my collarbone.

"Mess this up and you and me will have worse problems," he warned. "Got it, Nerd?"

I nodded while wishing I could climb into my back pocket.

Then the Bonebreaker leaned in to whisper, "Run behind Trayman. He's big enough to hide you until you get on Carolina's turf."

I nodded again and ran to Trayman just as Mr. Hicks blew the whistle to start the game. Naomi, plus five more from our team, joined us to create an offense that burst onto the field in one clump, then separated like a fan to create chaos. Bobby ran backward toward one wall of the gym so fewer people could get around us while I stayed right behind him, following his every move like a starving mosquito. Once we got close to the wall, Bobby's sneakers squeaked into a pivot toward the other team's jail.

"Keep up, Ned," Bobby said as I shadowed. "Here they come."

Carolina's defense suddenly noticed big 'ol Bobby had come too close for comfort. Six of her team rushed us as we crossed into their territory. A shout from Beck rallied our offense to keep Carolina's players away from us. Just before Bobby could be tagged by Beck's best friend, Richie Kaufman, Naomi sprang at him, tagged, and sent the second most powerful player of the game to my team's jail.

True craziness began when Carolina's team made another attempt to surround Trayman and me. How did I think this could work? More than half of our team was now in enemy territory! My days as Ned the Nerd were numbered; I would soon be Ned the Dead.

"Go!" Bobby gritted through his teeth before throwing a hand behind his back to shove me.

I fell, and Bobby accidentally stepped on my hand. I rolled

over and sat up just in time to watch Carolina tag Christopher.

"Spread out!" shouted Jared as if winning *Capture the Flag* was the only thing that could ever matter in life.

I threw myself onto my stomach and slithered away from further danger just as Rita and Max from Carolina's team bonked heads. They fell, blocking the rest of their team's path to Trayman.

Mr. Hick's whistle blew to freeze the action just as I reached the side of the puzzle mat cube. I sucked in a deep breath, slipped into jail ... and found myself nose-to-nose with Christopher.

As Mr. Hicks made sure nobody needed to head for the nurse, Christopher sneered, shaking his head in anger. "Can't believe I wound up in here before you, Nerd."

"Ned," I said before thinking about it.

But Beck's buddy didn't hear me over the whistle to continue game play. And he was too busy stretching his body as far out of the jail as possible so someone from our team could tag him.

"I got in here just like we planned," I raised my voice. "Nobody tagged me."

Christopher looked surprised. "Okay, good. Did you see their flag?"

"The basketball, right? It's next to the exit."

"Dude, that's a soccer ball."

It's round, it rolls. Who cares?

"If I move fast, I can get it," I told Christopher.

"Can you be fast?" He asked.

"I guess we'll find out," I muttered.

Just then, Mary showed up to tag Christopher out of jail.

"Grab their flag from the *left*," Christopher told me on his way out of the cube. "Their weakest player is posted there."

I glanced over at their weakest player, Tom, who suddenly noticed me in his team's jail. He shrugged sadly as if saying, "Yeah, what else is new?"

Suddenly, Jared Beck popped up in front of the jail in a rage. "Let's get two things straight: One, I hate your stupid little plan. Two, you stay in there, because I'm going for the flag!"

And just like that, Beck ran off to challenge Carolina's flag guards. The first guard he headed for? Tom, of course. Allow me to point out that when Beck runs after you, he resembles a T-Rex who just heard about the asteroid on its way to make him extinct. So Tom shook. Tom quaked. Tom ran away from the flag and joined me in his team's jail.

I ignored poor Tom and wondered if there was anything left for me to do: Apart from Beck's scheme, most of the action had moved to my team's territory. Three of Carolina's team stood in our team's jail, and four of our team guarded our flag, the orange cone. Offense and Defense for each team faked each other out by starting to run one direction, then reversing direction unexpectedly.

I glanced back at my target, the soccer ball, now guarded by only three people as they played chicken with Beck. The ball, from my angle, could be mine—*if* I were fast enough. *If* I were not too scared to defy Beck. *If* ....

I had one chance to run into the eye of the storm ... that calm place surrounded by chaos. So I ran on jittery legs—and tripped, falling onto my palms. Rather than attract attention by stumbling back to my feet, I snaked my way toward the flag, pulling my body along the floor by my elbows—a trick I learned during karate warm-ups. Sensei had called it the Army Crawl. Before I could believe it, my fingers reached for the ball, then ... Beck saw me.

His eyes narrowed, then popped and blazed like a cartoon

character drinking hot sauce. Of course, this drew the attention of the three flag guards to the guy on the floor behind them: little ol' me with one hand on their flag.

"Get him!" shouted Theresa before she dove at me.

My hands closed around the ball. I pulled my spindly legs beneath me, jumped up, and ran to get the flag into my team's territory. Theresa was right behind me. I could feel her fingers waving, reaching out, and just missing me with every lunge forward. Would she have caught me if the rubber on the toe of my sneaker hadn't stuck to the floor, propelling me forward? I'll never know.

My chin met the floor, the ball bounced ahead. Theresa tripped over me. Her teammate, Steve, tripped over both of us. Beck, however, pumped his body fast enough to veer around the whole mess toward the rolling ball. By now, Carolina's team forgot about trying to rescue their imprisoned teammates and five of them headed for Beck. But he caught the ball, dodged a tag from Carolina, and made it over the line to our territory.

Beck whooped, spiked the ball on the floor, and raised both arms in victory. He probably expected (as did I) that our team would clap him on the back and treat him like a hero.

But fifth graders aren't stupid; our team knew the plan. They knew I made it to the jail untagged. They knew my idea had worked and that Beck only carried the flag into our team's territory thanks to me. What they didn't know was how Beck tried to botch the plan.

Unbelievably, hand after hand landed on my shoulders as our team circled me. From the other side of the gym, Tom threw me a thumbs-up. Trayman nearly pulled my arm off by raising it as if I were just crowned heavyweight champion of the world. Just as I began to understand that the weird feeling running through me was pride and acceptance, Richie Kaufman shouted, "Hey! Wait a minute. Who tagged Ned in the first place? And who tagged him *out* of jail?"

"Nobody!" Trayman laughed. "That's the beauty of it. Ned pretended he got tagged. He put *himself* in jail. So he was free to come and go."

"It was Ned's idea," Naomi added with a sweet smile.

"That's cheating!" shouted Richie. "Mr. Hicks! Isn't it cheating?"

"Pretending you were tagged is not mentioned in my rulebook," Mr. Hicks said. "Such a strategy *is* pretty sneaky, so if you want to outlaw it in future games, I'm fine with that. But today? It's all fair and square. Clever strategy, Ned. Looks like you pay attention in history class."

"How so, Mr. Hicks?" asked Carolina.

"Remember the story of the Trojan Horse? The Ancient Greeks sent a giant wooden horse to the city of Troy as a peace offering during the Trojan War. The Trojans accepted the horse and brought it into their city. At night, Greek soldiers hopped out of the hollow horse and opened the gates to the city from the inside, allowing the entire Greek army in to conquer Troy. In a way, Ned acted as his own Trojan horse when he pretended to belong in jail."

"We should call the move the Herts Horse, as in, 'Yo! In yesterday's game, we pulled a Herts Horse,'" Christopher said, to my surprise.

"Yeah ... let's not," Beck sneered a warning at him.

Mr. Hicks placed a hand on Beck's shoulder. "Hey, Jared! Looks like your last pick for your team was your best pick."

"Ned's got the coolfulness going on!" howled Trayman. The rest of our team echoed his praise. Well, everyone except the team captain.

Judging from Beck's snarling expression and the way he glared at Christopher, my best strategy looked like my last. On the way out of the gym, I felt Beck breathe down my neck. "Some lucky break you had there, Nerd. But I can make your next break not so lucky."

Gulp. Just ... can't ... win.

CHAPTER FIVE

I went to bed that night in the black gi given to me by Tora Khan, hoping it possessed funky powers that would cause him to show up.

I wasn't expecting much.

Still, desperation had me talking to myself again. "Paging Tora Khan. Oh, illustrious Tiger King! I am in need of your wisdom."

Nothing.

"Dude, you don't know your hachikamas from hachimakis! Come defend yourself."

Somewhere in my house a toilet flushed.

"So I'm thinking of opening my own karate school tomorrow and telling everyone who shows up that the great Tiger King taught me *everything* I know. Care to comment?"

I fell asleep while listening for stealthy footsteps. When I woke, it was two o'clock in the morning. I hopped out of bed and kicked my school backpack across the room.

"So ..." I whispered loudly, "I'm probably going to die tomorrow by way of broken bones, embarrassment, or both—if anybody in the martial arts business cares!"

And ... nothing.

I pulled out my hachi-thing-a-ma-bob and tied it around my head. Slowly, quietly, stealthily, I opened my bedroom door, then crept down the hallway to the staircase. Step by step, I tried not to make them creak. Silently moves the ninja through the back alleys of this world's most feared hives of evil. He is practically invisible as he seeks justice, seeks—

A heavy sigh erupted behind me when I reached the kitchen back door.

"I thought you were deaf," I told my aged pooch.

Crack Jack's eyebrows flinched as if insulted.

"Go back to bed," I pointed toward the living room.

Cracker Jack began the pee-pee dance.

"No. You get your walk at six thirty."

My dog brought his big sad eyes two steps closer, then continued his dance.

Palm on forehead, I growled, "Where's your leash? Leash, boy!"

Mr. Skippy Paws happily lumbered out of the kitchen to get his leash.

Great. Some ninja. I can't even sneak out of the house without bringing my doggie with me.

Cracker Jack returned, leash in mouth, tail wagging. Oh, well. I'll probably be in a full body cast after Beck gets through with me in school. Might as well take my old pal for one last walk.

Cracker Jack looked nervous when I crossed the border between our yard and the woods. Normally, I would agree with him at this hour. But I wasn't nervous. In fact, I was sort of mad.

"Okay, Tiger King. Quit messing around. I need a move—one

move to bring down Beck tomorrow. Hello?"

We walked further. Cracker Jack peed, turned, and tugged at his leash, suggesting we go home.

"One move!" I called. "That's all I'm asking."

Cracker Jack whimpered, reminding me that we were alone in the woods, past midnight, with only weak moonlight to guide us. He had a point. Suddenly, fear did grip me. The last time I walked through here in the dark, Tora Khan was with me. And who would mess with him?

Should I turn back? Of course. Why was I out here, anyway? Oh, yeah; I was ticked.

An owl hooted. A breeze moved tree leaves. Funny how those sounds seem louder when you stand alone in the dark. Before I knew it, my feet froze in fear and my overactive imagination churned.

Leaves rustled again and convinced me a family of Big Foots was stalking us. I know what you're thinking: 'Ned, don't be a nerd. Why would Big Foots hang out in a small wooded area in suburbia?' But think about it some more; can you prove they don't?

Okay, so maybe a pack of wild dogs caused the creepy sound?

I pulled Cracker Jack closer. Poor guy wouldn't last a second if attacked.

Could it be cannibals? A gang of bank robbers using the woods as a hideout? Killer bees? Superheroes who switched to a life of crime? What if alien bugs living on a small meteorite fell through our atmosphere without burning up and landed in this area? And what if they decided to take over human brains? Egads! Could I become victim number one? I had to get out of there!

I yanked on Cracker Jack's leash and took off the way we came, frantically wondering how to protect myself if worse came to worse. I mean, after a handful of karate classes, what did I really know?

Panicking, I thought, kata. Isn't that supposed to help me out against thirteen people? Oh, what were the words again?

Bow, use your hammer, shield, uh.... Wait! Strike him, grab him, throw him to the ground! Every time I imagined doing that to Beck, I saw him standing like a mountain, laughing as I tried to throw him to the ground. But what else did I have?

We continued toward my house with me muttering, "Strike him, grab him, throw him to the ground. Strike him, grab him, throw him to the ground. Strike him...."

Cracker Jack stopped short and sniffed the air, causing me to trip over his arthritic butt. My own butt hit the ground while my shoulder slammed into a tree.

"Cracker Jack!"

But Cracker Jack stared up at the treetops, whining. Leaves rustled louder and louder as if they were ... wings? Birds? The dark-green leaves turned darker in the moonlight, then black. Not birds. *Bats!*

The bats were on us before I could stand. Cracker Jack took off. Panic gripped my heart, but it also brought me to my feet. I couldn't run, though; wings whipped around me while thin screeching pierced my ear drums as if the bats were just as frightened. Either that or they were vampire bats arguing over whether to bite my neck and make me one of them!

Words snapped into my head, and I screamed them in jaw-trembling panic while I attempted to do the moves: "Strike him, grab him, throw him to the ground. Strike him, grab him, throw him to the ground. Strike him, grab him...." I struck nothing, grabbed nothing, threw nothing to the ground. So I scrunched my eyes tight and kept striking, grabbing, and throwing unsuccessfully. Frantic bat wings slapped at my head and shoulders. It seemed as if nothing would stop them, and I began to think they were arguing over who got to snack on me first. Finally, I collapsed to the ground, arms over my head.

Then, without warning, the beating wings slowed and the screeching faded, replaced by the sound of something whipping through the air. Using my hands like a visor, I opened my eyes to see Tora Khan whipping a pair of nunchucks above my head. Speed made the wooden sticks barely visible as they whizzed around like helicopter blades. I dared not stand for fear of losing my head. I don't think I breathed until the last of the bats took off toward the tree tops.

"Herts!"

I jumped to my feet, shaking like a palm tree in a monsoon. Tora Khan whipped the chucks over his shoulder, threw them in front of himself, then caught both ends in one hand. He tucked the nunchucks into a regular leather, hold-your-pants-up-belt as Cracker Jack pawed the ground at his feet.

"Stop screaming," came the Tiger King's command.

But I couldn't. Bats carry rabies. They had been in my hair. They could have turned me into a creature of the night. I felt around my neck, checking for bites.

"Herts!" Tora Khan threw something at me.

I held out my hands. A warm package of aluminum foil fell into them. I stopped screaming. I pointed at the package, but couldn't yet speak.

"Taco," said Tora Khan.

CHAPTER SIX

A taco? The man had been incommunicado for two weeks
and he showed up with a taco? I needed advice,
superhero-quality moves ... a plan for surviving tomorrow.
He wasn't even in his gi this time. Instead, he wore a black
shirt tucked into blue jeans, a mini silver motorcycle for a
belt buckle, and black boots that could probably kick
someone from here to Tokyo.

A warm, spicy smell tickled my nose. I unwrapped the foil,
mouth watering over something my mother would never

approve of eating in the middle of the night.

Tora Khan held up a hand. "Wait," he said, then sat on a boulder. "How does a boy genius make the half-witted decision to wander the woods alone at night? "

"I brought Cracker Jack," I tossed back with a shrug.

Tora Khan's gaze turned to the trees. "Did you learn nothing from my daughter's last class?"

"Um ... huh?" How did he know about Sensei Melissa's lecture on putting oneself in unnecessary danger? Did he write her lesson plans?

"And the taco is better defense than this dog," the Tiger King said.

My growing shame over entering the woods alone transformed into anger. "Is that what you want me to do with this thing? Defend myself? I wouldn't even be here if you had shown up days ago. Where have you been?"

Tora Khan patted his hands around on his clothes as if he lost something.

"What are you doing?" I asked.

"Searching for the contract you think I signed to show up whenever your gi pants get in a twist. "

I pouted over his snarky comeback. "How about my hachikama? Is that in a twist? Because you got the name all wrong. This," I pointed to the cloth around my head, "is called a hachi*maki*. Sensei Melissa corrected me, and she's right; I looked it up."

"Of course, you did," Tora Khan said. "Hachimaki is correct."

Was that all he had for me? I had forgotten how little this man said unless you pulled it out of him. "So you, what? Forgot the correct name?"

"Your sensei called it a hachikama when young, so I often make the mistake myself. I keep my daughter with me in this way, as she was, with pigtails and bows, with me as her best friend."

"Aww," I said without thinking. "That's kind of sweet."

"Yes," Tora Khan said. "And then you all grow up." He reached down to scratch Cracker Jack between the ears, and my pup nuzzled against his hand.

"Martial artists do not invite trouble, Ninja Ned. They deflect it when it falls upon them."

"So you're saying I invited a nest of bats to swarm me by coming out here alone."

Tora Khan simply stood there with no expression.

"What would you have done if swarmed by bats?"

"Not your crazy dance."

"That crazy dance was kata."

Tora Khan whistled.

"What?"

"Thanks to you, hundreds of Grand Masters just rolled over in their graves."

"Ha. Ha. Thanks to you, so did hundreds of comedians. You couldn't see that I tried to strike, grab, and throw the bats? Seisan, you know."

"More like a hula with squirrels down one's pants." With a wave of his hand, The Tiger King dismissed my attempt at kata. "Not even necessary for a few bats."

I couldn't believe it. "What?" I ran a hand through my hair. "There were hundreds of them!"

Tora Khan raised one eyebrow.

"Okay, dozens. There were dozens of them."

"Try four that hardly came near you."

"They were in my hair!"

"When not in control of thoughts and emotions, it is possible to lose one's grip on reality."

"But they were—"

"At least five feet away. You felt the motion of their wings disturb the air near your head."

"If that's true, then why did you come at them with the nunchucks?"

"To scare them further off."

"Because they could bite me, right?"

"No. Because nobody wants to deal with the kid that peed his pants."

"Oh." Yeah, that would have been bad.

"Martial arts trains you to control thoughts and actions. Remaining calm in a crisis comes with experience and rank."

"Well, thanks for scaring off the bats. But I hope you didn't hurt them."

The Tiger King took an impatient breath. "Not one wing."

"You're annoyed. I can tell," I said. "I'm probably keeping you from something important." Game of chess? A good fight? A Nerd Protective Services meeting?

"Did you think yourself capable of handling a stranger in the woods who means you harm?"

I rolled my eyes. "Message received already—loud and clear. But if strangers are what you're worried about, I shouldn't step out of my house ever. Plus, I'm more worried about being taken out by a certain bully than I am a stranger."

"Martial artists prepare for any situation. But just because we are prepared to fight, doesn't mean we must or that we should. You learned that in your schoolyard when you merely stepped out of the way of Jared Beck's fury. In the end, his anger and lack of control only wounded himself."

Tora Khan's unusually long speech surprised me, and I thought back to the moment in the schoolyard when I took one step to the left, out of Beck's way, leaving him to face-plant on the concrete. But hold on: I narrowed my eyes at the Tiger King. "Hey, how did you know I did that?"

"Unimportant," Tora Khan said impatiently. "You used intuition. That is what matters."

"Well, I had to try something. But stepping out of the way won't work again. The next time Beck the Bonebreaker comes after me, he's going to be madder than ever."

"Because?"

"Because I had a better strategy than he did in gym."

"You showed him up," Tora Khan cracked half a grin.

"I guess?"

Tora Khan took a step toward me, and in the time it took to blink, had returned to his spot. Except ... my taco was gone.

"You're catching flies, Herts."

"You took my taco!"

"Speak the truth to yourself about yourself. Then you are worthy of the taco."

"Huh?" I mean was I really in the woods after midnight arguing over Mexican food with a martial arts master?

"Did you or did you not show up your bully?"

"I might have—"

"Wrong."

"I did show him up?"

"Sounds like a question." Tora Khan glanced up at the moon.

I took a breath. "I *did* show him up."

"Certainly. Why not take credit?"

Speechless, I shrugged.

"You allow others to decide how you think of yourself."

"I do?"

Tora Khan's features took on an expression of 'well, duh!'

Then he said, "Other people make a bad scale for judging oneself."

I kicked at a tree root. "It doesn't matter, because either way, I can't win. If I trip over my feet, I'm embarrassed. If I make a winning move, looks like I'll get beat up."

Tora Khan tossed the taco back at me. "Maybe, maybe not."

I reached under a bush to retrieve the foil packet after it sailed past me. "Oh, that's great," I called back at him while trying to avoid the sharp pine needles. "*Maybe* I'll need a body cast, maybe not. *Maybe* I'll need plastic surgery, maybe not. Maybe ..." I pointed a finger back at the Tiger King as I slid out from under the bush with my taco, "*Maybe* I'll become a vegetable after a punch to the head, maybe not."

The Tiger King raised an eyebrow.

"And with my luck? I'd wind up as celery."

He just stared at me. Maybe he didn't know the deal with celery.

"Get it? That's the worst sort of vegetable because, according to my mother, it is the vegetable that absorbs the most pesticides. As in, it's the most toxic vegetable? Nobody wants to be toxic. It's also the most boring vegetable. Nobody wants to be boring."

The Tiger King said nothing.

"As opposed to cabbage—one of the least toxic in the veggie family. But being cabbage has its own problems. You don't want to be around someone who ate too much cabbage, if you get my meaning." I pinched my nose and waited for a reaction ... which never came. I rested my case: "Nobody wants to be the main ingredient in a fart."

The silent warrior cleared his throat. "I meant, maybe you get beat up, maybe you don't, but a martial artist prepares for all outcomes. Preparation becomes confidence. Confidence becomes courage.

"I am prepared," I insisted. "I would like a blue body cast. I want to look like Bruce Lee if plastic surgery is in order—"

"Your actions and reactions change how people react to you. You teach people how to treat you. Changing your mind about yourself changes others' minds about you. Such change is never by chance; it comes from mental and physical action. Celery is toxic and boring because it has no choice but to be so."

"I can't change the fact that people find tripping over things and knowing the answers to every math question funny."

"Ah, but do you trip and get up meekly or do you take a bow? Do you hide behind your intelligence or use it with pride?"

Take a bow? Was he serious?

"Look people in the eyes, Ninja Ned. When someone stares at you, stare back. When they mock you, keep walking, head held high. If they come at you with fists—"

Suddenly the Tiger King did! I scrunched my eyes shut and threw my arms into a double block. His fist was like iron against my forearm, but I cast it aside, shocked that Sensei Melissa's blocking drills had come in handy. I hadn't even thought about blocking the punch; it just happened.

"Now, Ninja Ned, do you see how ability grows?"

Rather than feel pride, triumph, or hope over my natural reaction to Tora Khan's attack, a horrible feeling attacked my stomach. Because it wasn't just my fear of winding up in a body cast that made me dread going to school or simply walking down my street. No, not even close.

"Jared Beck's words hurt—sometimes worse than when he trips me in the hallway," I blurted. "How do forearm blocks, fist blocks, or x-blocks stop *that*? They don't!"

Tora Khan took a deep breath, and hope filled me. Clearly, he was about to give me the answer I needed! Everything was going to be okay because a great karate master was about to solve all my problems. He said:

"Herts. Eat your taco."

Maybe it was the lump growing in my throat, but my first bite of the taco was revolting. Mushy. Nearly tasteless.

"You block his words by not accepting them, Herts. Recognize his words as gifts not to your taste—do not accept them. What you do not accept does not belong to you; it still belongs to the giver. Allow Jared's words to fester within himself, while you remain free."

I managed a second bite of the taco. "I have to tell you: I sort of regret accepting this taco."

"Bland, isn't it?"

"The blandest."

"Texture?"

"Mushy. No crunch."

"Worst Mexican food in town!" the Tiger King said with pride.

"Um ... thank you?"

"You're welcome."

"Why would you do that?" I said, re-wrapping the taco.

"Oh, no. You're going to finish that," Tora Khan said.

"Why?"

"Because it's part of tonight's lesson."

"And that lesson is, what? How to vomit like a ninja? How to emit a poisonous gas cloud from my backside to immobilize an opponent or desecrate this entire forest? You know, Beck's going to torture me enough tomorrow. I don't need to spend all day running to the toilet."

"Lions will spook a herd of gazelles and watch how they react before targeting the slowest and weakest members of the herd first. Bullies do the same."

"You're telling me?" I peeled my lips back to take another small bite of the taco.

"Karate challenges you to move faster and build strength. Those physical skills grow over time through dedication, but you can use your mental skills now. You proved capable of doing so in gym class."

"I don't know ..."

"How did your classmates react to your winning strategy?"

"They cheered." The corners of my mouth lifted as far as

they could go over the memory.

"What if they became aware of *all* your unique qualities—the ones you keep buried? Imagine their surprise."

As I digested Tora Khan's words, I worried over how my stomach would digest the taco. I held it out to Tora Khan.

"You want a real surprise? Have a bite."

"Military strategists study their enemies to find weaknesses in their plans, in their armor. They provide their soldiers with such information—it's called intelligence—so they can fight their best fight. Sounds as if you're smarter than Beck. Analyze him: What is he afraid of? What does he get from messing with you? Whatever it is, don't give it to him at your expense."

"You're my Yoda, aren't you?" I blurted.

Tora Khan's blank stare returned. The man needed a crash course in pop culture, for sure.

"Hey, get this, TK: Beck's mother wants me to tutor him."

"Oh," said Tora Khan, rising from the boulder. "Don't do that."

"I don't plan on it. Tutoring Beck would certainly be walking into unnecessary danger. That would—"

"I meant don't call me TK. But don't tutor Beck, either."

My teeth met something weird in the taco. "Hey," I stuck a finger into the mush and fished out a ... plastic baggie? I dropped the taco and held out the sauce covered bag. Something flat was inside. I unsealed it, knelt to wipe my fingers on grass and pine needles, then pulled out a thin stack of narrow paper rectangles.

I couldn't believe it: They were tickets to *Rallington Comic Fest!* Four tickets. Four tickets that sold out weeks ago!

I looked up at Tora Khan, but he was gone. I didn't need an explanation, though. The disgusting taco held two lessons inside: 1) Look past the bland and mushy; you never know what surprises it may hold. 2) We can find some good, even in the most unappealing situations, if we look for it.

"Thank you!" I called out toward the moon.

In my head, I heard, "Use the fourth ticket for the girl."

CHAPTER SEVEN

Normally, English is the class that challenges me least.
As a reader and writer, I absorb words and ideas like a
four-eyed sponge. That is, when I don't have vats of taco-
infused gas swirling in my stomach and when I'm not
dreading what Jared Beck might do to me at recess. On the
flip side, I felt the giddy excitement of knowing I had tickets
to *Rallington Comic Fest* and that Tora Khan had suggested I
'use the fourth ticket for the girl.' Had he meant Adrianna? Of
course, he had! It's not like I had girls falling at my flat feet.

But *how* would I ask her to go?

With all that going on in my stomach and head, I was supposed to write poetry, which I dislike very much. Still, I scribbled the beginnings of poems worse than the cheesiest greeting card on page after page in my notebook. The assigned subject? Something important going on in my life.

First, I tried focusing on Adrianna:

For every punch and every kick your tiny limbs express,
To your right, is a heck of a guy ... but he's really just one hot mess.

Sigh.

Then I thought writing about fear would make me one of those dark and brooding poets. You know, the type who writes stuff people feel in their souls—yet the guy would probably be a bummer to hang out with at a dinner party:

The bully strikes with teeth and claw,
He likes to eat Godzilla meat raw.
I had thought he'd be in jail by the ripe old age of four.
I was wrong.

Blah, blah, blah.

Then I thought, maybe my work should be uplifting:

Rainbows, birds, skunks, and flowers,
I could watch nature for hours and hours.

But that work of poetic genius just made me want to beat myself up.

My stomach growled, that swirling storm of gas talking taco once more. Hmm....

Out of all superheroes far and wide,
Gas Man throws a weapon that aims from behind.
Give him a taco, give him a ham,
Give him some beans, and suddenly ...
BAAAAM!

As if I needed my first 'F' in English? Stupid taco.

Or maybe it wasn't so stupid after all; the taco reminded me of Tora Khan. Finally, the poet in me came out:

The Tiger King roars silently,
before the break of day.
He stalks the forest stealthily,
with nothing in his way.
He fights the darkness fearlessly,
until the sun's first ray.
Watch ...
Duck ...
as a bladed-star soars.
Blink and you'll miss it,
when the Tiger King roars.

Finished, with ten minutes to spare. Not bad, Herts. Not bad at all. In fact—

"Ned Herts, please gather your belongings and report to the Guidance office," came the school secretary's voice over the PA system. "Ned Herts to Guidance."

That was unexpected. Still, I handed in my poem, threw my backpack together, and headed for Guidance.

Ms. Shoemacher, the fifth-grade Guidance Counselor, sat behind her desk—across from Jared Beck.

"Hello?" I said, my backpack hitting the floor much like the stone in the pit of my stomach.

Ms. Shoemacher beamed as if giving me the best news of my (soon to be shortened) life. "Ned, I have a service project for you."

No. No. No, no, no, no....

"Jared needs a little extra help in a few subjects, so his mother requested a student tutor. And she suggested you!"

Right about then *I* needed a lot of help with English.

"Consider this an honor, Ned. It's also a wonderful opportunity for you and Jared to work together toward a common goal. I'm sure you'll become a great team."

Great team? Oh, yeah. I mean we've worked together for years! Scenes from my past played out in my head: Ned and the Bonebreaker demonstrate how to hang a nerd by his winter jacket from a coat hook. See this one-of-a-kind team entertain the lunchroom with side-splitting antics such as Ned and his lunch tray flying over Beck's foot. Watch Ned wiggle-dance after that ever-clever King of Comedy, the Bonebreaker, sticks a pencil—point first—down the back of Ned's shirt while changing classes.

What happens to adults that makes them forget life as a kid? How could Ms. Shoemacher or anyone else not realize the crazy bad in this tutoring idea?

"I thought you might try two days a week during lunch and a couple of mornings before classes start," Ms. Shoemacher said with a smile that suggested everything was right with the world.

I forced my lips to move. "I ... I ... have to check with my parents first."

Ms. Shoemacher's smile grew impossibly wider. "That's all set, Ned. Your father thought it would be a wonderful challenge for you."

Challenge? I challenge Dad to remember who caused him to lay out money for karate lessons.

I stole a look at Beck. The moment Ms. Shoemacher

glanced down at her calendar, he threw me a toothy grin. This was not going to happen; the minute I got home I would set my parents straight.

Ms. Shoemacher straightened her glasses and stood. "I thought you might start today. You can eat lunch here in the Guidance lobby with Mrs. Gorman. Perhaps help Jared with tonight's math homework?"

My head jerked up and down as if forced by a puppeteer.

Jared let out a sweet and overly drawn out, "Suuuuuure. Sounds good, Ms. Shoemacher. I can't wait to teach Ned ... ehem, have Ned teach me some lessons."

I do believe my stomach and lungs just switched places.

So there I sat at a table in the Guidance office, eating my bag lunch while waiting for Beck to return with something off the lunch line. My sandwich—turkey and cheese, sprinkled with wheat germ—had no taste. Then again, I had no appetite. By the time Beck returned with a burger and tater tots, I had given up on eating.

"So where do we start?" Beck asked too enthusiastically. He pulled out a notebook and some math sheets.

I scanned the pages. Fractions—my favorite. No, really!

"Okaaaay," I squeaked. "What don't you understand?"

"Huh?" Beck popped a tater tot, then chewed with his mouth open.

"What do you need me to explain?"

Beck leaned in and whispered, "How about you explain why you haven't started filling in the paper yet?"

"I ... I'm not supposed to do it for you," I stammered.

"You sure are," he sneered.

I craned my neck to catch the secretary's attention, but Mrs. Gorman must have stepped out.

"Don't even," Beck growled, then placed a pencil in my hand.

I sucked in a breath. "So if we have to reduce two-fourths, we should—"

"Just slap in the answer, Nerd."

"What happens when ... when you have to take a test?"

"I'll fail it."

"But then—"

"Then you will look like a lousy tutor." Beck's eyes sparked wide with glee.

"But—"

"But what, Nerd? You upset you'll miss recess hanging here with me? You don't do anything fun, anyway."

Actually, Tom and I had plans to step beyond our social status and ask the girls if they wanted to play *Capture the Flag*. My last performance in gym had both of us feeling a shred of confidence. Right now, one of two things was happening in the schoolyard: Either Tom was running around like a real lady's man, or he was sitting alone by the fence doodling a new costume design for one of our superheroes—a man forever married to geekish pursuits.

I reduced the first two fractions on Beck's worksheet, then put down the pencil. "You know, if you're not going to do the work—"

A spit ball stung my cheek.

"Stop!" I gritted through my teeth.

Beck's foot swept around the back legs of my chair and he pulled upward, tilting me so I had to fight not to slide off the chair and under the desk.

"Stop!"

"Pick the pencil back up, Nedso."

I looked around once more for the secretary. Nobody. The chair tilted steeper.

Military strategists study their enemies to find weaknesses in their armor, Tora Khan had said. *They provide their soldiers with such information—it's called intelligence—so they can fight their best fight.*

I locked eyes with Beck. Why was he doing this? What made him so mean?

Maybe he needed a good hug from his mom instead of insults? Although, she did care enough to get him tutoring, didn't she?

More of Tora Khan's advice came back to me: *What does he get out of messing with you? Whatever it is, don't give it to him.*

I still didn't know what Beck got out of messing with me, but whatever it was, I didn't have to give it to him. I pushed the paper and pencil away and tried to ignore the rage building in Beck's eyes. "So this next one is the same thing. First you look to find the—"

He pushed the paper back at me. "*Do it.*"

The secretary returned, heels clicking rapidly. Slowly, Beck eased my chair back onto four legs. He leaned in closer. "Put in the answers if you know what's good for you."

Heart racing, anger building, I coughed loudly, then repeated my instructions for the next problem. I just kept talking through however many glares Beck threw at me. Soon he started ripping paper from his notebook and sending me notes. He wrote some dooseys:

"You should go shopping, Nerd. Maybe you can buy yourself a personality."

"Maybe I shouldn't underestimate you, wimp. After all, you could single-handedly bore the whole world to death."

"The main office is out of rubber bands. Maybe they can use your legs."

It took time to read these gems since the spelling was so horrible and the handwriting worse. In the middle of another fraction problem, I pulled over one of his scraps of paper and wrote, "Please write in English. I can't read Martian."

Beck's foot swung around my leg and pressed the ankle bone against the metal chair leg. "Hey Four-Eyes, don't get brave. You'll wind up with more problems than the ones you'll have in Science."

Now that worried me. Science was my next class. But Beck wasn't in my class. What would happen in Science?

My ankle throbbed. I tried to pull away, but Beck's brute strength forbade it.

"Mrs. Gorman!" I called. "Do you have an extra sheet of paper I could use?"

Sweet Mrs. Gorman waddled over to us with a smile on her wrinkled face and a stack of copy paper instead of one sheet. No wonder the school budget was in the toilet. Beck backed off quickly, so she didn't see what he was doing to me.

I moved my feet as far from Beck's as possible.

"Science!" he snarled as Mrs. Gorman waddled away.

"What?" I asked.

"You'll get yours in Science. How nice of you to leave that

gift for Mr. Nizzlo, Ned. When he gets back to his classroom from lunch, he's going to be so surprised!"

My eyes opened wider than the frames of my glasses.

"What did you do?" I breathed.

"Me?" Beck touched his chest, his face full of mock surprise. "No, Ned. It's what *you* did."

Sounds as if you're smarter than Beck, Tora Khan had said. *Analyze him.*

What would Beck leave in a classroom? What would Beck *do* to a classroom? Nothing good.

I drew in a breath and rose to my feet. "What did you do?" I asked again.

"I've been here all along, Nedsy—stuck in here with you. Good thing I've got a bunch of friends who don't mind sneaking out of the lunchroom. How about you? Got any friends willing to help you out of a biiiiiig mess?"

The huge office clock told me I had fifteen minutes until lunch was over. Without another word, I threw out my lunch, grabbed my backpack, and ran out of the office.

CHAPTER EIGHT

S neakers squeaking, I ran the hallway to Mr. Nizzlo's classroom, ducked in the door, left the lights off, and took in a terrible sight.

Uh-oh. Oh, no!

A snowy forest of toilet paper streamers hung from the fluorescent light fixtures, across bulletin boards, from the flagpole, and from clotheslines of science project reports that ran criss-crossed throughout the room.

My heart drummed deep in my chest as if prepping to

NED THE NINJA: HEAD IN THE GAME

explode. I dropped my bags at the back of the room and jumped to reach a streamer. I was too short. Well, really, how would Mr. Nizzlo think I did this, anyway? I was his best student. He would never suspect me.

Then I saw it: On the whiteboard, in huge black letters, someone had written:

REMODELING BY NED HERTS

This stuff had to come down! I stepped onto a chair, then on top of a desk to reach the bottom of a streamer. I grabbed and tugged. Pieces of toilet paper fell to the ground. Carefully, I stepped back onto the chair, then down to the floor to head for the next desk.

Wait a minute. Did I need to clean this mess? I ran to the whiteboard and used the eraser to get rid of the phony evidence. Nobody could blame me without this note—

Nothing happened.

Permanent Marker! They used permanent marker?

Think, Herts! The clock above Mr. Nizzlo's desk said I had

nine minutes left to save my reputation. I climbed onto another desk, reached for more paper, tugged, and only succeeded in tearing off the bottom. So I—me, Ned Herts—jumped while on top of a desk, more fearful of a mark on my school records than cracking my head open on the floor. And when I jumped, I managed to strike the paper with my hand hard enough to knock it into more toilet paper strands beside it. I grabbed, pulled, and down came a bunch of streamers.

Eight minutes.

I eyeballed the distance between me and the next desk, finding it wasn't much farther than distances I've jumped in karate class. My heart raced. My mouth dried up enough to put the Sahara Desert to shame. I stuck my feet side by side, bent my knees and tuck jumped forward.

My feet nearly landed on the edge of the next desk, but I managed to shuffle to the center before physics tipped it. I jumped straight up, struck a wad of TP streamers with the side of my hand, grabbed them, then threw them to the ground.

Jump *over!* Jump *up!* Strike 'em, grab 'em, throw 'em to the ground!

I moved from desk to desk, gaining speed.

Over! Up! Strike 'em, grab 'em, throw 'em to the ground!

Over! Up! Strike 'em, grab 'em, throw 'em to the ground!

When I had cleared toilet paper from the last of the light fixtures and the clotheslines of reports, I hit the floor and ripped more streamers off the bulletin boards.

Four and half minutes.

My name still taunted me from the board, and the floor looked like the boys' bathroom, so I set my feet atop a pile of torn toilet paper and shuffled around the classroom, gathering the stuff in front of me in an ever-growing pile. Finally, I trashed it and faced the board.

Four minutes!

I ran to one of the computers and hit the Internet to search for a solution. Immediately, I found a home tip article that said dry erase markers would remove permanent marker.

They can't be serious. It sounded too easy.

Running out of options, I grabbed a black dry erase marker

and scribbled all over the incriminating evidence. Then I found a roll of paper towels—thank goodness Beck chose to torture me in a science classroom—and got to work rubbing out the letters.

It worked! I couldn't believe it.

Score one for the nerd!

When the whiteboard was white again, I stood back and looked for anything I missed.

One minute to spare, or so I thought; the side of Mr. Nizzlo's head appeared at the back door of the room, bobbing and nodding in conversation with someone. But his hand rested on the doorknob; I knew because it jiggled as he leaned on it.

A bell rang over the PA system. Lunch was over. Soon the halls would crawl with students. I turned to sneak out the front door of the room, hoping whomever Mr. Nizzlo was speaking with would block me from view. But just as I turned the doorknob, I happened to glance at the back of the room one more time. And—

Uh-oh. Oh, no!

There, where I missed it, right smack in the center of the wall, hung a sheet of paper impaled on a coat hook. It read:

MR. NIZZLO SMELLS LIKE CHEESE FARTS.

SINCERELY,

NED HERTS

The doorknob turned as Mr. Nizzlo finished his conversation, his head still turned away from the door. I wouldn't have time to make it to the paper that insulted my favorite teacher! My breath came in short bursts as a desperate idea popped into my head. I scanned Mr. Nizzlo's desk for something, anything I could make fly.

One wild grab gave me a DVD about the *Periodic Table of Elements*. I aimed. I focused. I chucked that DVD like a throwing star.

It hit the paper with enough force to rip it from the hook.

As the paper fell, the doorknob turned all the way. I dropped to the floor. Using my arms to pull myself along, I Army Crawled to the window side of the classroom. My legs dragged behind me, barely making a sound. I, Ned Herts, became stealthy, and if I wasn't so terrified, I would have been proud.

The lights flicked on, and Mr. Nizzlo's shoes tapped across the floor, making their way along the opposite side of the room toward his desk. By then, I had nearly reached the back of the room. Only I would have to move straight across Mr. Nizzlo's line of sight to get to the back door. I raised my head. He was reading something on his desk. So I gulped a breath and tried to imagine I looked like a bold, deadly snake as I slithered across the back of the room. On my way, I slid the fallen paper with me. I would just have to hope he didn't notice my backpack. Finally, I pulled myself into a crouch and snuck out the open back door.

Trying to breathe, I leaned against the hallway lockers and folded the 'cheese farts' paper a million times before tucking it in my pocket. Then I eased back into the classroom with three other students, including Tom, quickly grabbing my backpack on the way to my seat.

"Whew! What's with you?" asked Tom. "You look like you've

been to war." He slid into the seat next to me. "Did you narrowly escape death or something?"

"Close," I whispered as Mr. Nizzlo moved in front of his desk to greet arriving students.

"Hey," Tom giggled. "Don't look now, but Mr. Nizzlo's got toilet paper stuck to his shoe."

CHAPTER NINE

Hi Adrianna. Want to come to a convention with me? What kind? Er ... the kind where people wear costumes honoring their favorite comic book characters and movies? See you could wear a mask and nobody would recognize you.

Uh, no.

Hey there, Ade, How's about coming with me to pick up some of the best fandom swag this side of the country?

Dork.

Yo, Adrianna! It's your lucky day. I have tickets to watch nerds parade around in costume and stand in line for celebrity autographs.

Well, now that one just made me angry. What was I? Some kind of sellout? Shame on me, taking a shot at my people. If Adrianna didn't want to experience the glory of geek culture, her loss. If she couldn't appreciate and celebrate the creativity and imagination behind the world's best films and comic books, then I would just have to find my soulmate elsewhere.

But still....

Oh, Adrianna with the orange sherbet hair! Would you accompany me to a convention, thereby making me the happiest man ... boy ... in the world? I found the tickets inside a taco.

Oh, barf.

Hey, girl. You. Me. Comic book convention. Pick you up tomorrow at 8:00 am.

Way to get slapped, Herts.

I picked up my giant first-aid kit and bowed into the dojo where Adrianna sat stretching alongside the rest of our class. Oh, forget it. I could never ask her.

After placing my bag along the far wall, I dropped to the floor beside Adrianna and tried to reach for my toes. They remained as far out of reach as the possibility of me showing up at a comic book convention with a girl.

"Hi, Ned!" Adrianna said excitedly. But she always spoke that way. Everything seemed exciting to Adrianna—one of the reasons I liked her.

"Hey," I said shyly. My cheeks heated with the memory of all the invitations I had practiced.

Sensei Melissa walked into the dojo. Immediately, each student jumped up and bowed. She bowed back.

"Good evening, everyone. Keep stretching. We have five minutes before class starts."

Then she headed straight for me.

Uh-oh. Oh no! What did I do?

"So Ned. You go to Pascack Brook Elementary, don't you?" I nodded.

"Mr. Hicks and his wife are friends of mine. We went to college together years ago."

"He's my gym teacher," I told her.

"Yes, I know. I met them for dinner last night, and he told me about this kid named Ned Herts who pulled a brilliant Trojan Horse-style stunt in *Capture the Flag*."

My cheeks burned like twin suns.

"So I'm thinking, *my* Ned Herts? And sure enough, he described you."

"What did you do, Ned?" asked Adrianna.

"I ... uh ... threw myself in jail. So I could get out of jail whenever I wanted. Nobody had to free me because nobody tagged me in the first place. So when I suddenly went after the flag, nobody expected it."

Sensei Melissa nodded enthusiastically. "Mr. Hicks said Ned pitched the whole game in another direction, allowing his team to win. He was blown away by Ned taking such initiative in gym class."

No mention of Jared Beck bringing the flag over the line. No mention of him being captain. Just me. They spoke about little old me.

"That's thinking outside the box, Herts. You should feel proud." Sensei held up her hand in a hi-five.

I jumped to slap her hand. "But," I pointed out, "What I did will probably be illegal from now on."

"So you'll come up with something new next time. You're

good at using your head, Ned."

"Yes, Sensei,"

With a nod, Sensei moved to the front of the room to lead us in a bow-in.

"Awesome, Ned," whispered Adrianna. Her words filled me with oceans of confidence.

"Wait until I tell you what I had to do in my Science classroom. I was a total ninja," I whispered.

Adrianna giggled. "Ned the Ninja?"

"Yep," I whispered.

"Aswate!" came Sensei's command. The class dropped to its knees.

"Rei!"

We bowed, heads close to the floor.

"Tatte!"

We stood, hands at our sides.

"Dorchester! Who tied your belt today?" Sensei asked good-naturedly. "It would be right if you stood on your head."

While Sensei dealt with Dorchester, I leaned toward

Adrianna and whispered, "I have tickets to the *Rallington Comic Fest* tomorrow. Want to go?"

For a while, Adrianna said nothing, her eyes on Sensei. In fact, she said nothing throughout jogging in place and squat thrusts. I thought it was over. I blew it. I got too confident. I was lucky a girl like Adrianna even said 'hello' to me, and there I went asking her to hang out.

But just as we dropped to the floor for sit-ups, Adrianna whispered back, "Sure. What time?"

"About ten in the morning. Do you like comics and movie fandom stuff?" I asked.

"I don't know," she giggled quietly. "But I'm sure it will be fun either way."

"First drill!" came Sensei's command. "On the floor, face down, arms at your sides. For each count: Jump into a fighting stance, throw two rear kicks with the last kick advancing into a spin-around backhand punch. Finish with a jumping roundhouse. Got it?"

I so did not have it. Still, for the next five minutes, I threw my whole self into that drill. I fell on my face twice trying to jump from the floor and tangled my fist in Adrianna's ponytail before I could backhand punch. In fact, if you ask me, anyone who avoided getting smacked in the head with my roundhouse kick should be given a free pass to their next rank. Still, each time I ran the drill, I got better. Maybe not as quickly as someone else would. But I wasn't and never would be someone else. I was and always would be Ned.

I decided to steal a glance at Adrianna through the mirror. I wanted to see if she looked upset that I pulled her hair. Instead, out of the corner of my eye, I saw a stealthy reflection flash past the doorway from the lobby. Black gi, gray hair—it was the Tiger King!

I turned, stepped off my dot, and craned my neck to see if he was in the lobby. Nope.

"Herts?" came Sensei's voice.

"I think I saw your father," I blurted without thinking.

Sensei, hands on hips, raised her eyebrows, then pointed to the wall of pictures that included one of Tora Khan. "Well, yes. He's right there."

"Yeah, but—"

"Herts!" Sensei's voice boomed. "Is your head in the game?"

"Yes, Sensei," I said, trying not to smile. "Yes, it is."

"Good, because it won't be long before you need to prepare for testing."

"Testing, Sensei?" I forced a tremor out of my voice.

"For your yellow belt. I have no worries about you being ready by testing week. Do you?"

"No, Sensei!" I replied, having no idea when or what testing week was.

So I returned to the drill, building speed, building strength ... building confidence in who I wanted to be ... building the courage I wanted others to recognize in me ... building ... Ned the Ninja.

THE END

(... until Book Three)

ABOUT THE AUTHORS

Kea Alwang lives in New Jersey with her podcasting husband, film-obsessed son, and book-munching daughter. Apart from writing and world building, she teaches Isshin-ryu karate, searches for the perfect chocolate bar, and immerses herself in multiple fangirl obsessions.

Her other works include the Young Adult Speculative fiction series, *Based on a Dream*. Find Kea online at: www.keaalwang.com, www.basedonadreambooks.com, and www.infiniteinkauthors.com.

Melissa Mertz owns and operates *The Dojo Paramus* in Paramus, NJ, where, as a 5th level Black Belt in Isshin-ryu, she has taught for over ten years. She is forever grateful for the opportunity and privilege of teaching martial arts to those who have trained with her. She thanks her students and their parents for their trust and for following her path to Black Belt. Melissa lives in New Jersey with her star-throwing son and the sweetest dog the world over.

36370595R10071